First published in the United States and Canada in 1996 by North-South Books,

an imprint of Nord-Süd Verlag AG, Gossau Zürich, Switzerland.

Distributed in the United States by North-South Books Inc., New York.

Copyright © 1993 by Michael Neugebauer Verlag AG, Gossau Zürich, Switzerland

First published in Switzerland under the title LebKuchenMann *by Michael Neugebauer Verlag AG*

English translation copyright © 1993 by Picture Book Studio Ltd. London

First published in Great Britain, Australia, and New Zealand in 1993

by Picture Book Studio Ltd. London. Reprinted in 1996 by North-South Books.

Library of Congress Cataloging-in-Publication data is available.

British Library Cataloguing in Publication Data is available

ISBN 1-55858-542-7 (trade binding) 10 9 8 7 6 5 4 3 2 1

ISBN 1-55858-543-5 (library binding) 10 9 8 7 6 5 4 3 2 1

Printed in Italy

The Gingerbread Man

An Old English Folktale Illustrated by

John A. Rowe

A Michael Neugebauer Book / North-South Books / New York / London

Once upon a time in a little old house,
there lived a family of mice.

One day, mother mouse decided to bake
a Gingerbread Man for her children.
She mixed the dough, cut him out,
and popped him into the oven.

After a while she went to the oven
to see if the Gingerbread Man was ready.

But as she opened the oven door,
the Gingerbread Man jumped up and ran away
as fast as he could, laughing and singing,

Ha ha ha, hee hee hee,
I'm the Gingerbread Man
and you can't catch me!

Mother mouse chased after him,
but she couldn't catch the Gingerbread Man.

So he ran and he ran, right through the garden
where father mouse was busy digging up carrots.

"Who are you?" called father mouse.

And he answered,

**Ha ha ha, hee hee hee,
I'm the Gingerbread Man
and you can't catch me!**

Father mouse chased after him,
but *he* couldn't catch the Gingerbread Man either.

So he ran and he ran, right across a field
where the mouse children were playing.

"Who are you?" called the mouse children.

And he answered,

**Ha ha ha, hee hee hee,
I'm the Gingerbread Man
and you can't catch me!**

The mouse children chased after him,
but *they* couldn't catch the Gingerbread Man either.

So he ran and he ran, till he came to
an old hedgehog taking a rest.

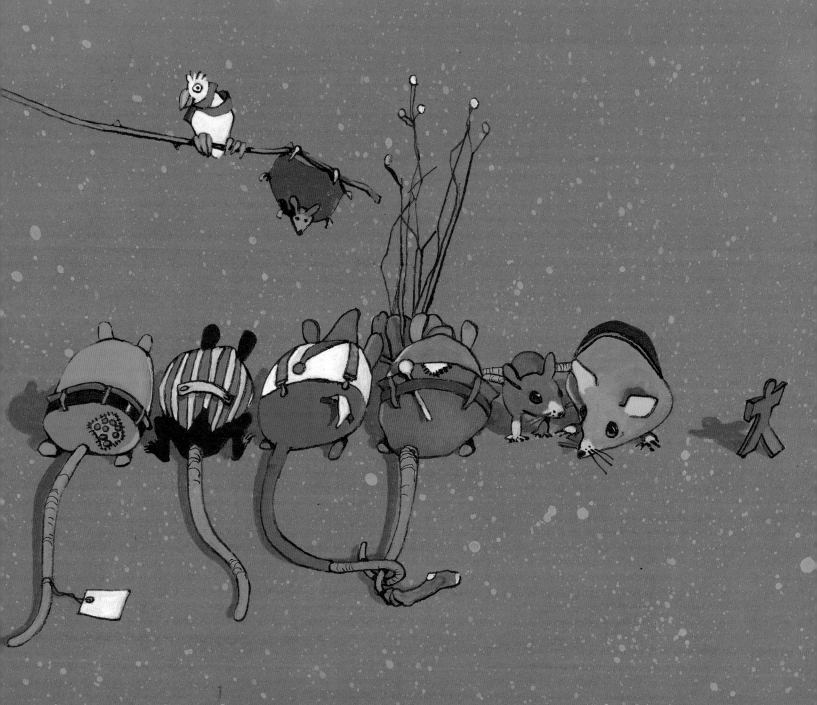

"Who are you?" called the hedgehog.

And he answered,

Ha ha ha, hee hee hee,
I'm the Gingerbread Man
and you can't catch me!

The hedgehog chased after him,
but _he_ couldn't catch the Gingerbread Man either.

So he ran and he ran, till he went past a hill
where two beetles lived.

"Who are you?" called the beetles.

And he answered,

Ha ha ha, hee hee hee,
I'm the Gingerbread Man
and you can't catch me!

The two beetles chased after him,
but _they_ couldn't catch that Gingerbread Man either.

So he ran and he ran, till he came to
a hare asleep in the grass.

"Who are you?" mumbled the sleepy hare.

And he answered,

**Ha ha ha, hee hee hee,
I'm the Gingerbread Man
and you can't catch me!**

The hare woke right up and chased after him,
but *he* couldn't catch the Gingerbread Man either.

So the Gingerbread Man ran and he ran, and soon
he came to a fox lying beneath a tree next to a river.

"Who are you?" asked the fox, licking his lips.

And he answered,

**Ha ha ha, hee hee hee,
I'm the Gingerbread Man
and you can't catch me!**

The sly old fox just laughed and said, "If you don't get across this river soon you *will* get caught. Why don't you climb onto my tail and let me carry you across?"

The Gingerbread Man saw that the river was too deep and that he had no time to lose, so he climbed up onto the fox's bushy tail.

"Oh dear," said the cunning fox. "The water's getting much deeper. Why don't you climb up onto my back so that you don't get wet?"

So the Gingerbread Man climbed up onto
the fox's bony back.

"Oh dear, oh dear," said the hungry fox. "The water's even
deeper now. Why don't you climb up onto my head so that
you don't get wet?"

So the Gingerbread Man climbed up onto
the fox's furry head.

"Oh dear, oh dear, oh dear," said the fox. "The water's much
too deep. Why don't you climb up onto my nose so that you
don't get wet?"

So the Gingerbread Man climbed up onto
the fox's quivering nose.

Then suddenly, with a quick flick of his head,
that sly old fox tossed the Gingerbread Man up into the air,
and he caught him with a snap of his jaws.

And *that* was the end of the Gingerbread Man!